MAD DOG ™
IN THE
BIG CITY

MAD DOG™
IN THE
BIG CITY

Written by Leslie McGuire

Illustrated by Steve Haefele

HOOKED ON
PHONICS™

ISBN 1-931020-00-0

Contents

Contents

Special Words

Special words help make this story fun.
Your child may need help reading them.

city

eye

nose

1. Good Is Boring!

Mad Dog wiped his feet on the carpet, banged the lamp with his tail, and said, "Not one fun thing has happened lately. I need something to do today that's really, really fun! I need to go on a trip! Besides, I am sick of being good."

Mad Dog had been very good for a very long time. But he had not always been good. There was a time when he was very bad. He used to puff his chest and jump in junk. He chomped car tires. He smelled like skunk.

He liked to stand on cats and roll in fish. He liked to run off with the kitten's dish. Cats do not like that sort of thing.

But then Mad Dog turned into a good dog. He kissed the cats. He had lots of baths. He played with dolls.

But today was different. Today there was an odd spark in his eye. His tail was a bit too waggly. His grin looked a bit too sneaky. His ears looked a bit too perky. It did not look like a good day for cats.

Mad Dog was planning on taking a trip. He just needed to pick where he wanted to go! But going just any place was not what he wanted. He needed to think.

"I could go to the forest and catch bugs," he said. "Nope! Too dull."

"I could go to the lake and chase frogs," he said. "Nope! Too silly."

He was thinking very hard. Then he said, "I could go to the big city and..."

But then he stopped and said, "Nope. Too far away!"

Mad Dog sat down on the grass by the road. It was hot. He was bored.

He just wanted to have a little fun, but having a little fun was hard!

The one thing he could think of that was fun was going to the city. But Mad Dog needed a ride to get there.

Just then, a big clunking truck pulled over under a tree at the side of the road. Two men got out and ate lunch.

One man said, "Hurry up and finish!
We need to go quickly to that big job
in the city."

Mad Dog said, "I know what I have
to do! I know a way to get to the city!"

He could hide in the back of the
truck and ride all of the way!

17

All he had to do was jump in
without letting the men see him!
   They got back in the truck. They
could not see Mad Dog. Mad Dog
looked this way and that way. There
were no other people on the road.

Mad Dog put his ears back. He
flopped his belly down on the road.
He snuck up on the truck as carefully
as he could. He got past the men.

But he could see that getting into
the back of the truck was going to
be hard.

It was too far up to jump!

That's when Mad Dog saw a big log.
He gave it a push. He could stand on
it and jump into the back of the truck.

It was a good plan.

But then the truck started up.

"Oh no!" he said. "I will never make
it in time!"

2. In the City

Just as the truck was starting to go,
Mad Dog hopped on the log and
made a flying leap. He shut his eyes.

"Please, please, please, let me make
it," he whispered to himself.

He landed with a plop on a pile of ropes and tires. Mad Dog hung on as the truck zipped down the road. The wind flapped his ears, but Mad Dog did not care. He was on his way!

The trip was long, and Mad Dog had a good nap tucked in with the tires. He was dreaming about rolling in a big, smelly pile of trash, when suddenly his nostrils began to twitch. He did not know if he was dreaming or not.

That was when he woke up. There were cars all over. The air was filled with smoke. There were trash cans and puddles all over. There were cats and dogs and people. There were hot dog stands and stores and buses. The truck kept hitting potholes, and Mad Dog was popped from one side of the truck to the other. But he did not care. He wanted to see everything, but the truck was going too fast.

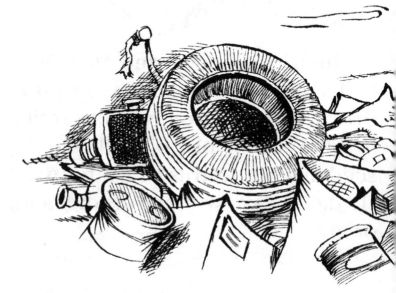

Mad Dog waited until the truck stopped in traffic. Then he jumped off. He ran and hid in back of a pile of boxes. The truck turned a corner and drove away.

"Fun at last!" Mad Dog barked.

Five cranky cats were sitting on the boxes. When Mad Dog began to bark, their tails got stiff. But when they took a good look at Mad Dog, they did not like what they saw. They ran into a hardware store as fast as they could.

"Good," said Mad Dog. "Now for some fun!"

His ears perked up, and his tail began to twitch.

The hot dog stand down the street smelled very yummy.

"All I have to do is sneak up to the hot dog man and grab a bunch of his hot dogs," Mad Dog said to himself.

So he put his ears back, flopped his belly down on the pavement, and snuck down the street.

When the hot dog man was not looking, Mad Dog grabbed a big bunch of hot dogs.

But before he could get away, a hand grabbed his ear.

Mad Dog yelped. That was not fun. That hurt!

Mad Dog dropped the hot dogs. The man picked them up.

But as the man yelled, "Get over here!" Mad Dog ran off as fast as he could. The hot dog man ran after him! Other people ran after him, too!

"Catch that dog! Lock him up!"

Mad Dog ran as fast as he could, saying "This is no fun!"

That's when he saw stairs going down. A big sign said Subway.

"That's it!" Mad Dog said to himself. "I'm going down there right now!"

He tore down the stairs just as five hundred people came up the stairs.

"Oh no!" Mad Dog yelped. "I am about to be flattened like a pancake!"

3. Lost Down Under

He got bumped in the side. His tail got stuck between shopping bags. He got slapped with a backpack. A little trunk got dropped on him, but Mad Dog made it down to the bottom.

That's when he saw a very odd, big, long train.

Just then, five hundred more people came up in back of him and pushed him inside.

"I hope this is fun," said Mad Dog.

The next thing he knew, he was in the train, and it was going very fast in a deep, dark tunnel. All of a sudden, it stopped, and about one hundred people pushed past him to get out. Mad Dog decided it was time to get out, too.

He went with the people up the stairs. Things did not look the same at all.

"This is no fun," said Mad Dog.

But at least there was no hot dog man.

"OK," said Mad Dog. "It's time for fun and snacks."

But Mad Dog checked all of the stores, and there was not one yummy thing in any of them. It was getting dark. It was getting late. Mad Dog was getting hungry. The big city was not so much fun right now.

Mad Dog was thinking about his snuggly bed and his big dish full of snacks. He wished he had on his fluffy slippers, and maybe his floppy hat with the bunny ears. He felt lonely and sad.

That's when he smelled a funny smell.

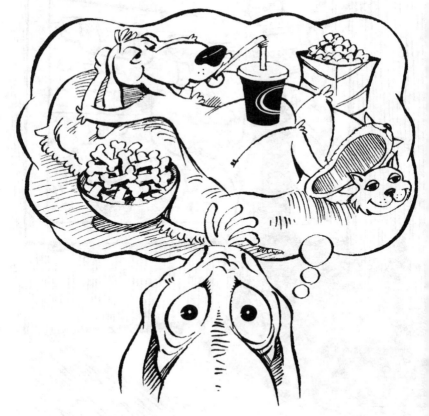

4. Did You Bake Me a Cake?

It was smoke.

"Did they bake me a cake?" Mad Dog asked himself. "Cakes are fun! Maybe I will check it out!"

The cake did not smell too tasty, but for now, Mad Dog did not care. Any cake was better than no cake at all!

But where was the cake smell
coming from?

"I will follow my nose," said Mad
Dog. He looked this way and that.
His nose twitched. He went up some
stairs. He checked in the corners.
The cake did not smell too good.
It smelled burned!

"They are burning my cake!" Mad Dog said to himself. He looked way up the stairs, and he saw lots and lots of smoke. Too much smoke! He started to run up the stairs.

This was not a burning cake! This was a fire!

"Uh-oh!" said Mad Dog. "I need to get help! It is very late. The people in here do not know about this fire! I bet they are all sleeping!"

He began to bark! He barked and barked. He rushed up and down the steps, barking as much as he could. People began to come outside. Then they began to yell. They grabbed pets and kids and ran outside in their bathrobes and slippers.

Mad Dog kept running up and down the stairs until he saw that all of the people were out and safe. It was getting very hot, and he could see flames, but he ran inside.

He got to the top of the stairs and stopped. He could hear soft barking.

"Why is that?" he asked himself. Then he said, "Uh-oh. Maybe a puppy cannot get out by himself!"

Mad Dog barked and barked, but no one came. He put his nose down by the crack in the door and barked some more. No one came.

"I must do something!" Mad Dog said. Then he came up with a plan!

At the end of the hallway, there was a window. Outside the window, Mad Dog could see a ladder. He ran to the ladder. He could see a porch with rails that went outside past all of the windows.

Mad Dog hopped out onto the porch and ran, looking in each window.

Then he came to one window and saw a puppy sitting on a bed. The window was shut, but Mad Dog did not care.

He kicked at the window as hard
as he could. It broke, and Mad Dog
jumped in. Mad Dog had a cut on his
leg, but he did not feel it. He ran to
the bed. He grabbed the puppy and
pushed him over to the window.

49

Mad Dog and the puppy jumped out onto the porch. Mad Dog looked down. It was going to be a much bigger jump than he wanted to think about.

Then Mad Dog could hear yelling. It was the firemen and all of the people. One of the firemen was climbing up a big ladder to get them!

5. It's Good to Be Good!

When Mad Dog and the puppy got down, all of the people wanted to hug and kiss them. The firemen said Mad Dog was the best and bravest dog they had ever seen.

Mad Dog barked to say, "Thanks, but now I am hungry!"

They did not seem to hear him.

Mad Dog had just saved a puppy!
But all of the people who lived
there said he had saved them, too!
His barking had gotten them up so
they could get out in time.

Mad Dog barked, "How about
a snack?"

They all smiled and patted him.

Mad Dog was a hero! The mayor
had him over for dinner.

"It's about time!" said Mad Dog.
"I need that big ham over there."

They gave him a dish full of dog
treats—but no ham.

The firemen had given him a big prize and a letter with all of their names on it.

"Can I eat this?" asked Mad Dog.

He was on TV ten times. No matter
where he went, people wanted to
hug and kiss him.

"That's good," said Mad Dog, "but
a snack would be more fun."

He went to party after party.

"This party is sort of fun," said Mad Dog. "But please pass the little hot dogs. I want that liver stuff, too. It looks very tasty."

They gave him a plate of Doggy Din-Din, but no hot dogs.

The hot dog man came up to him
one day and said, "Shake, buddy! You
are one brave mutt!"

"If I am so brave," said Mad Dog,
"then you could give me a big bunch
of your hot dogs."

He did not give Mad Dog anything.

It was not until a week later that Mad Dog got to go home.

"All I wanted was some fun," said Mad Dog. "Not only was it not that much fun, but they did not feed me!"

"Yes, they did," said the cats. "They gave you dog treats and Doggy Din-Din."

"Not very quickly," muttered Mad Dog. "Besides, I wanted some really good people snacks. People snacks are lots of fun!"

"But you were on TV," said the cats. "We all saw you!"

"That does not help when you are hungry," said Mad Dog.

"How come not one of the people got what I was saying?" Mad Dog said to the cats. "I got what they were saying! What's the matter with them? Can't they hear?"

"People are good," said the cats. "They give us warm spots to sleep in. They make yummy snacks for us."

"If they think of it," muttered Mad Dog.

"But they are not that smart," said the cats. "We have to help them. We have to show them how because sometimes they are a bit slow."

"Uh-oh," said Mad Dog. "It's hard to be a teacher."

"Not for smart cats or a smart dog like you," said the cats.

"How can I be a teacher?" Mad Dog asked.

"All you have to do is be good all of the time," said the cats.

"We can be good, so you can, too," said the cats. "Besides, being good is much more fun."

"That's true," said Mad Dog.

So here's what Mad Dog does these days.

He makes his bed.
He cleans his plate.
He does not stay up
Very late.

And every day when Mad Dog gets up, he says, "It's good to be good—and fun, too!"